Austin Stack

Dinner with Teddy

Bumblebee Books
London

A CIP catalogue record for this title is
available from the British Library.

ISBN: 978-1-83934-405-3

Bumblebee Books is an imprint of
Olympia Publishers.

First Published in 2022

Bumblebee Books
Tallis House
2 Tallis Street
London
EC4Y 0AB

Printed in Great Britain

www.olympiapublishers.com

Dedication

For Edith.

Sitting in a corner, sitting alone.
No-one outside, no-one to phone.

What shall I do till my dinner is ready?
All I can do is play with my teddy.

Teddy the soldier.

Teddy the clown.

Teddy goes up.

Teddy comes down.

Musical teddies, sitting on chairs.

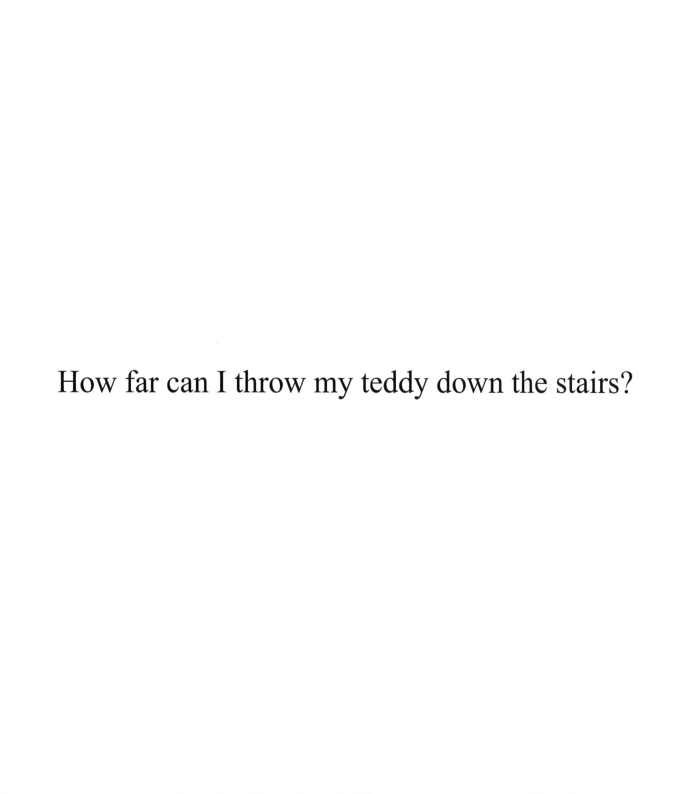

How far can I throw my teddy down the stairs?

Space-bear teddy travels the stars.

This book belongs to
_____

ISBN-10: 1699278679
ISBN-13: 978-1699278673

www.johnoboyle.net

Written by John O'Boyle

Cover art and original black and white interior illustrations by Mykita Harets
ngarets@gmail.com

Edited by Shannon Jade
www.wildflowerbooks.net

Thank you to Moira for the interior illustration colouring.

Mechanic teddy fixes old cars.

Doctor teddy makes sure you are well.

Magical teddy puts you under a spell.

Bedtime teddy is full of snooze.

Helpful teddy will polish your shoes.

Gardener teddy digs with a spade.

Grizzly teddy is never afraid.

What's that? Do I hear a voice from downstairs?

"Dinner is ready for children and bears."
I love when I hear that dinner is ready,
It's the best time of day for me and my teddy.

About the Author

Irish born, moved to England where he met his wife of over thirty years. Has owned a small-holding, worked as a carer for additional needs adults, and used to run a wool shop in Devon. Austin began writing stories for his children, and the recent birth of his first grandchild has inspired him to pursue publishing his work.

Acknowledgements

Thanks to Sara, May, Charlie, and Brad
for putting up with all my silly rhymes.

Printed in Great Britain
by Amazon

14579693R00025